D0099093

Caravan to the North
Misael's Long Walk

Caravan to the North
Misael's Long Walk

Jorge Argueta

Pictures by Manuel Monroy

Groundwood Books
House of Anansi Press
Toronto Berkeley

Groundwood Books / House of Anansi Press
groundwoodbooks.com

We gratefully acknowledge for its financial support of our publishing program the Government of Canada.

With the participation of the Government of Canada | Canadä
Avec la participation du gouvernement du Canada

Library and Archives Canada Cataloguing in Publication
Title: Caravan to the north : Misael's long walk / Jorge Argueta ; pictures by Manuel Monroy.
Other titles: Caravana al norte. English
Names: Argueta, Jorge, author. | Monroy, Manuel, illustrator.
Description: Translation of: Caravana al norte. | Translated by Elizabeth Bell.
Identifiers: Canadiana (print) 20190115610 | Canadiana (ebook) 20190115637 | ISBN 9781773063294 (hardcover) | ISBN 9781773063300 (EPUB) | ISBN 9781773063317 (Kindle)
Classification: LCC PZ73.5.A74 C3713 2019 | DDC j863/.64—dc23

Jacket and interior illustrations by Manuel Monroy
Map by Mary Rostad
Design by Michael Solomon
Printed and bound in Canada

To all the immigrants from Central America and Mexico, you are the true dreamers. To all the good-hearted people who generously help them along the path to the North. — JA

Acknowledgments

The author would like to thank the following people for their support during the production of this book: Héctor Jiménez López, Nora Obregón, Carolina Osorio, Alfredo Pérez, Holly Ayala, Yuyi Morales, Manlio Argueta, Xosé A. Perozo, José Ardón, Evelyn Arizpe, Juan Carlos and Hugo Fernando Osorio, and Patricia Aldana.

Us

My name is Misael Martínez.
I've come to join
the caravan
that's leaving tomorrow
from the Plaza Divino Salvador
del Mundo* to the North.
I'm going with my
family.

We decided to leave
because you can't really live
in my village anymore.
There's no work.
There's no way to get by.
What there is,
is violence, gangs.

* The name of this plaza in El Salvador's capital means "Divine Savior of the World."

Home

I love my country
so, so much.
I love to plant
the fields,
see the corn come up
and the little beans sprout.

Every year in May
the whole family
gets the land ready
for planting.
We do the weeding, fertilizing.
We pray for a good crop
and when the first rains fall,
we get up before sunrise.
We feel happy when
we put
the best of the corn and the beans
in our Mother Earth.

My papá says,
"There's nothing prettier
than watching the first
blades of corn poke up.
It's the cutest thing
to see it come up bright green and grow.
We raise the crop like it was a child."

"Yes," my mamá says.
"This is what we have.
We are good with it.
We get by
until our time is up.
Ahhhh,
but now and then
we cook a wild hen,
we make tamales and then
we feel fat and happy."

But here in our village
things are all screwed up now.
I tell them:
"In the schools
the gangs want
us to join them.
We can't walk down
the street.
They stalk us.
It scares us.
We're sad."

"We can't cross the street.
We can't go from one barrio to another,"
says my brother Martín.
"Because this is one gang's turf,
and over there it's another's."

Our friend
Juan Yegua's son
disappeared.
They say he got mixed up
in stupid stuff.
Gang stuff.

"I don't know
anything about that,"
my mamá says to us.
"But what I do know is
they're just pups.
They're children like you,
the kids who get caught up in that,
and they turn into bad guys,
I mean really bad.
Even murderers."

My mamá looks
at my brother Martín and then at me.
There are tears in her eyes.

Then she speaks
again:
"I feel sorry for them
because they're kids
from poor families.
They're the poor
screwing the poor.

"Those poor babies,
those kids
in the gangs,"
my mamá says,
crying …

"They leave their homes
and then they're nobody's children.
They're the gang's.
The gangs are their family.
It scares me
to even say this.
It's their law here:
See. Hear. Be quiet," she says.

"A few days ago,"
my papá says,
"it was Martina's son.
I don't know the whole story,
but I know
the police came
and the kid ran away
and they shot him.
He was a child, just
about to turn
sixteen.
The people who saw him
say the boy was begging,

'Don't kill me, please don't kill me.
Don't kill me,' he was saying.
Poor kid died crying
and calling for his mamá.
As a dad, that really hurts,"

"I'm scared, Papá.
I'm scared, Mamá."

I told them I heard
there's a caravan
that's leaving
from San Salvador
to go to the United States.
I tell them we should go.
We all say, "Let's go."

Mother Earth

When the gualcalchillas*
sing,
my heart sings
and I know
our Mother Earth's heart
is singing too.

* A gualcalchilla is a little yellow songbird with a voice as loud as an orchestra.

———

Plaza Divino Salvador del Mundo

So many people
in the Plaza
Divino Salvador del Mundo,
and how beautiful it looks.

Everyone says
they want to leave
for the same reasons:

The violence.
No work.
They've lost
hope.

Some don't want to go.
Their parents are taking them or sending them.
The kids don't know where they're going.
They just get taken.

"I'm from Sonsonate."
"I'm from Chalatenango."
"I'm from La Unión."
"I'm from San Salvador."

"We came
to join the caravan
that's going to the United States.
We want to go there, we want to work,"
says a man
with a green backpack.
He touches it and says,
"This is full of hopes."

A skinny curly-haired boy,
angry and sad, says,
"I sell fruit in the Central Market
but you can't live on that here.
It hurts to see my parents.
They're old now.
I want to help them out.
I'm nineteen.
Got my high school degree
but now I can't go on
with my studies.
I want to get my education and help
my parents, that's why I'm leaving.
I came to join the caravan.
You can't study here
or work.
On a good day
I make ten dollars selling tomatoes and onions.
My heart is always asking,
'What are we gonna eat today?'"

A woman with her arms around
her daughter says in a shaky voice,
"My guts are twisting
but even though it scares me
to leave, it's better to go.
I want a better life."

"Yes," another woman says.
"We came to join the caravan
because when you're alone
the road north is dangerous.
In the caravan
we help each other."

Some boys
say happily:
"We come from Ciudad Barrios,
the land of the saint and prophet
Óscar Romero.
We're going to Mexico.
After that, we're not sure
but we're going.
We're like
birds looking for
a new dawn."

"Yeahhhh!" some other boys say all together.
"It's too much here.
That's why
all of us are leaving
in the caravan. It's not as dangerous.
We're going to the North
with our mamás and our papás
and our brothers and our sisters."

In the Plaza Divino Salvador
del Mundo
my mamá says,
getting it off her chest,
"It's true, here in El Salvador
you can't get by.
We've tried.
I've looked for work.
They won't hire me.
These boys make me brave.
I'm going to get
to the United States."

"These boys
are my life.
They're going to go to school.
They'll have
what I didn't.
We're going to make this happen."

"I love El Salvador so much,
but here
you can't live.
There's no work.
I don't want to leave
but I don't know what to do.
Ayyy — I'm so worried," my papá says.

"Me too, I'm taking
these two brats,"
says a man in a hat,
a man from San Vicente.
"I want
my sons
to graduate from high school, so they can go on
to college.
Here, when you finish high school
you end up
selling water
on buses
or in parks,
or if not, God knows what they'll do.
Nooo, I
want my sons
to have dreams,
and to have their dreams come true!"

"I love El Salvador,"
says a man
who is praying,
looking up at the sky.
"I'm a widower
with two daughters,
Margarita and Juana.

"I love El Salvador.
But here
they don't love us.
We are poor.

"You can't live
on promises.
Ayyyyy —
El Salvador! It hurts me so much,"
he ends, crying.

A little girl running happily
around the plaza says,
"My daddy is bringing my stroller.
They say the North is really far
but my daddy is strong.
He's going to push me
and play games with me
and with the north wind too."

Another little girl says,
"My mommy kisses my face.
My mommy makes me laugh.
My mommy sings to me.
My mommy gives me a yummy pupusa* for dinner.
My mommy holds me in her arms."

* Pupusas are the national food of El Salvador, round cornmeal cakes filled
  with beans, cheese or meat.

Here in the Plaza
Divino Salvador del Mundo,
we sleep all bunched together.
The grass is as green
as my parakeet's wings.

One little girl holds a doll.
She's happy. She says,
"My doll Josefina and I
like to go to sleep watching the stars
while Mommy holds us in her arms."

We Set Out

Before the sun comes up
we set out walking.
We set out by bus.
We set out by truck.
We set out.

Divine Savior of the World,
saint of all Salvadoreños,
help us on the road, guide us.
Take us away from here, make a miracle.
Carry us away from here, even though it hurts.
Help us to get far away,
far, far from El Salvador.

Now we're going.
Who knows when we will come back?
I look around me
and see the volcano of San Salvador,
the city and its buildings.
The Divine Savior of the World.
I'm going to miss El Salvador so much,
especially now with Christmas coming.

What I'm going to miss most about El Salvador
are the snow cones.
I think about the mangoes
and the marañones.*
Ahhhhh and also the jocotes.†
They taste so good.

* Marañones are the colorful fruits of the cashew tree.
† Jocotes are delicious tropical fruits. Their name derives from the Nahuat
word *shúgut*.

Now it's five in the morning
and we're leaving.
It's better to walk
at dawn. It's not as hot.

I look around me
and the sky is still kind of dark.
There are hundreds of us.
Some are crying,
others laughing nervously.
They're praying, singing and saying,
"We'll get there!"
I'm sighing, I'm shaking,
not sure if it's from happiness
or cold or fear.

We're walking.
The sun of El Salvador warms me.
I like feeling the sunshine.
My backpack's a little heavy.
I think about how far
the North is.
We're barely going to reach Santa Ana
and I'm tired.
El Salvador is big.
How about Guatemala?
And Mexico?
To say nothing of the North?

Sometimes all you hear are footsteps
of people walking —
tran tran tran tran —
as if we were marching,
or as if we were
horses.

The streets are a long, long black road.
We're going toward the border
of Guatemala. I'm tired but happy.
The pavement is hot.
We have a long way to go
before we reach the North.

Waking Dreams

When we get there,
I'm going to have an apartment
with water you can drink.
I'll bathe in warm water
and have a washing machine.

"I just want to work
and send money to my mom.
She's really old and has no pension,"
says a boy
who is walking by my side.

"I'm going to start college.
Maybe I could be a lawyer
or a teacher or a doctor.
Well, I'll settle for just getting there
and then we'll see," says another boy.

Caravan

"I just hope
my shoes hold up," says
a lady, and she laughs.

Some have taken buses
to get farther ahead.
Others would rather keep
the little money they have with them.
You have to eat along the way.

I sold my computer
and my cell phone.
Matilde bought them from me.
No way in the world
would she leave El Salvador, she said.

Now that we've started
on this caravan,
I wish I had my cell phone
to take pictures.
I never left
my town before.
El Salvador is beautiful.
What a shame
that we have
to leave.

We're crossing the border.
"This river is called Peace,"
my papá tells me.
I look at the water running
silently and slowly.
I want to turn back,
go back to El Salvador.
My papá is looking forward.
He says to me
in a happy voice, "Over there
is Guatemala,
and then Mexico,
and farther on,
the United States,
where we are going to live."

I breathe deep and look at the sky.
I think about Christmas
on its way
and all the mamás
who came to say goodbye
and were left alone crying
in the Plaza Divino Salvador
del Mundo.
The mamás who couldn't come
but sent their children.

Some men
and women in the caravan
say they're going to go
toward a town
called Arriaga.
They say a train
passes through it
called The Beast.
It makes me kind of nervous
but it doesn't matter
if we're going.
We're going, no matter how.

We are in Chiquimulilla.
Stone-paved streets,
people watching us walk by.
They greet us with smiles
and wave at us.
Women and men
dressed all in colors.
They look so beautiful.
They look like birds.

They give us water and food.
The smiles that people give us
taste best of all.
I wear my scapular
and a fist of courage in my heart.
Nothing can stop us.

We'll sleep here tonight
and early tomorrow, again,
we'll go on.
I'm tired.
I hear voices
saying names
of towns and cities
I've never heard of before.
Zacapa,
Tecún Umán,
Tapachula,
Mapastepec,
Querétaro,
Irapuato.

I'd like to hear
the name of my friend
back in El Salvador.

For over a week
we've walked.
We've ridden in trucks
and buses.
We've slept in parks, in streets
and in shelters.
In some places
people are glad to see us, they help us.
In others they chase us away.
I don't know where the North is.
It's like they pull it away, or hide it.
I don't care anymore.
Sometimes
I'd like to close my eyes
and be back at my house, in the yard.

In the caravan
we've walked
I don't know how many kilometers.
Some say thousands.
In caravan we've cried.
In caravan we've sung.

The cold is so cold.
Mexico City
is icy
but the buildings
are so pretty
and the tacos
are so delicious.
The ones I like best
are the fried pork tacos.

Walking and Remembering

I wonder about my house —
the walls,
the windows,
the shadows,
the trees —
everything that
I don't have anymore
but that has built a nest
in my heart
and sings *torogoz torogoz*
torogoz torogoz.[*]

* The national bird of El Salvador, the torogoz has a striking, repetitive call.

"Watch out for hawks,"*
says a man.
I look up in the air.
I want to see them flying.
I can only see threads
of rain
falling
from the top of the sky.

* Hawk (*halcón* in Spanish) is a slang term for a human trafficker.

I'm happy
in Mexico.
A man at the shelter
tells us stories.
I like them.
They make me happy.
The story
about the wind —
nothing and no one
can stop it,
no one can see it —
you only hear
zuuummmmm laugh
zuuummmmm sing
zuummm zuuummm.

Another man
we call
el carnal*
because we like him.
He makes us pupusas.
"The pupusas are ready,"
he tells us.
He stands on a chair
in the shelter
and cups his hands
like a microphone
and calls really loud,
"Come get your pupusas!
Pupusas filled with dreams,
pupusas filled with rainbows,
pupusas filled with song,
pupusas filled with love."

Mmmmm. The pupusas
are a little square
but delicious.

* Carnal is slang for friend.

It keeps raining
in the shelter yard.
I watch the rain.
In every drop
I see my friends,
my relatives,
the streets of my town.
The rain
makes me shiver.
I sigh and cover up in a blanket
next to my mamá
and my papá and my brother Martín.

In a few days
we're going
to Tijuana.
It's not that far
from here.
"I'm staying there,"
says one lady
from Guatemala.
"They say there's work.
They've got nice beaches.
They speak English,
and if you decide to go on
to the real North,
it's just a step away from Tijuana.
I like that and I'm tired
and so are my kids."

Christmas All of a Sudden

Christmas took us by surprise
in the shelter.
I didn't even realize
it was Christmas already.
I miss the burst
of fireworks
and hugs all around, *ummm,*
and the chicken stew
and the posadas.*

<hr />

* In the Latin American tradition of posadas, groups of people go from house to house, replicating the journey of Joseph and Mary, asking for shelter. The groups sing as they go and are sometimes received with gifts or piñatas, and sometimes turned away.

Walking in the caravan
reminds me of the posadas
and that song that says,
"In the name of Heaven
I beg you for shelter …"
Here we're all walking,
asking for shelter.

Some women
have come from the shelter.
They've made turkey for us.
They have books, they read to us
stories and poems.
They also bring us piñatas
and candy and little presents.
We're all happy
with the piñatas.
They're red and blue and yellow
with green fringes.
They remind me of the kites
we used to fly in my town.

Voices from the shelter
rise and fall.
Sometimes I feel sadness.
Sadness makes me sad.
Now I know, sadness
is like not seeing, not hearing.
It seems like everything stops,
even the air, even the North,
and your heart leaves you
sigh by sigh.
I'd better sing
and keep dreaming.

Almost There

Tomorrow we're going to Tijuana.
Some buses and trucks
are coming to take us
to Tijuana.
"Tijuana is no-man's-land," Don Agustino shouts.
"What does that mean?"
I ask him.
"It's that Tijuana
is sort of a bridge.
There are people from all over the world.
It's like a port.
It's like an airport.
Even people who live there
speak English."
"Ahhh!" I say, but I don't understand.
I look at the sky.
The freezing rain keeps falling.

On the road
to Tijuana,
we pass through Querétaro.
"It's beautiful,
all the colors and the stone,"
my mamá says.
"Can't we stay here?
There's so much peace here.
Is there work, too?"
she asks, sighing
through the bus window.

I distract myself
watching the cars
and the buses go by.
The wind whistles
and the rain
never stops.
Tijuana is
so far away.
It feels like it's
as far away as
El Salvador.

In the back of the truck
some people are silent.
Maybe they're praying.
Maybe they're tired.
Maybe they're scared.

The name Tijuana
is kind of funny to me.
Maybe it's just my nerves, but
it sounds like "Tía Juana." *

* Spanish for Aunt Juana.

Back at my house
no one waits for me.
We're all here.
My papá, my mamá
and my brother.

I think about good things.
Those nice ladies.
The Santa María patronas,[*]
the patronas
all made of
love and sweetness,
then I'm not lonely anymore.

---

* The patronas are rural Mexican women from Guadalupe (La Patrona), in
  Amatlán de los Reyes, Veracruz. For over twenty years they have given food
  and water to migrants traveling on La Bestia, or The Beast, also known as the
  Train of Death.

On the bus
a Mexican man
starts singing,
"I've come back from where I was …"
We all know
the song,
and we sing,
"Fate allowed me to return …"
The bus is named
El Ausente — the Absent One —
like the song
José Alfredo Jiménez sings.

I fell asleep.
I don't know how much
time has gone by.
A Honduran man,
Don Miguel, keeps saying excitedly,
"Tijuana, Tijuana, Tijuana!!!"

The bus
comes to a stop.
The driver
says,
"Ladies and gentlemen,
we have arrived in Tijuana."

Tijuana

Ufff.
At last we are here, in Tijuana.
It's filled with lights.
The lights are beautiful
like stars, and there are so many buildings.

But it's so cold here too,
and raining so hard.
First they brought us to a shelter
but it was leaky.
Everything got all muddy.
It reminds me of the downpours
in El Salvador,
except there
the rain was warm.

The children cuddle up
in their mother's arms
like baby chicks.
They're cold and they're coughing.

We'll be going to a different shelter,
the Mexican authorities tell us.
I'd like to go back home.
I'm tired.

They say that in the United States
the cold is colder,
but who cares?
I've already made it and gone through the worst.
I'm going forward,
we're going forward.
We're going to get to the North,
wherever it is.

In the shelter
some Mexican men and women
brought us
toilet paper, diapers for the babies
and other supplies.
This night we eat really well —
beans, eggs, tortillas and bread.
Everything is nice and hot.

Tonight I'll sleep in peace.
From here it's only
a little bit farther to get to the North,
and here in this new shelter
it's not as cold, there's not as much mud.

Suddenly there are screams,
shouting and crying,
and a strong smell of pepper.
It wakes us up.
"What's happening? What's happening!!!???"
asks my brother Martín.

"There's chile in the air,
in the air,"
he keeps saying desperately.
"What do we do?
What do we do?"

"Close your eyes,
close your eyes!!!"
We hear desperate
screams
from men and women.

The children cry and cough.
The smoke is a black cloud.
It covers the whole shelter.
We cover our heads with our clothes.
We pour water on our faces, we're cold,
the water is cold, but it helps.

Little by little, things calm down.
We can only hear murmurs
and sighs. No one knows
who it was.
We just know it was
tear gas.

"Like we were at war,"
says a lady from San Salvador.
"I lived through the war in the eighties
and that's how the national guard attacked
the student demonstrations.
It's horrible, it's sad.
We're not criminals, we're migrants.
We just want to get to the North.
We want to work."

People pray
and hug their children.
"How awful, how sad,"
I say when I hear
what the lady said about
our countries,
that they persecute us.
And in the North they don't want us.
What are we to do?
Where are we to go?
Ahhh, I'm just going
to sleep,
praying and watching
the rain fall.

To Cross the Wall

"At dawn we're leaving.
We're going to cross
the border.
We will be in the North
once and for all,"
my mamá and my papá
say firmly.

That's what we all feel
in the caravan.
Everyone wants to get to the North.
Everyone is tired.
Everyone wants to go to the wall and cross over.

A Honduran kid
says in a loud voice,
stirring up the whole caravan,
"Tomorrow we will cross the wall,
tomorrow we get to the North!!!"
"Yessss!!!" the voice of the caravan
answers excitedly.

That night it is quiet,
just the wind blowing,
and when the rain dies down
you can hear some snoring
or migrants whispering to each other.

Morning comes fast.
We are waiting for it.
We are all nervous.
We are all on our feet.
We all want to go.
"Let's go north!!!"
a voice says,
and everyone answers,
"Let's go!!!"

Once again, we are walking.
We are heading toward the border,
toward the wall.
I can't wait
to get to the North.
I want all this to be over.

It feels like we're in the middle
of a bunch of poisonous snakes.
There are lots of people
shouting chants
against us.

They say we are criminals.
That we are drug dealers.
They say we are bad people.
I'm confused,
I'm scared.
My hair is standing on end.

In the distance I see the wall.
It's big, with barbed wire on top.
It has bars.
It looks like a huge jail.
"Uyyyy," I say.

The people keep yelling.
Some say that Tijuana
doesn't want us.
Others say
they'll give us work.
I don't understand.
I'm just scared.

I'm in front of the wall.
People are climbing it
and crossing over.
There are immigration trucks,
police with shields
and soldiers everywhere.
I'm really, really, really scared.

They shoot tear gas.
People are running every which way.
I hear screams
and wails.

My mamá takes my hand
and holds me.
My papá hugs my brother Martín.
"Run, we have to run!!!"
my mamá says.

Everyone is running.
Some are crying from the gas,
some are crying from sadness.
Finally we get
far enough away.
We're near the sea.

I see the waves break
and roll north,
and no one
says a word to them.
The waves, like the North, the wind,
can go where they want.
If someone were a wave …
If only I were the North, the wind.
If only all the migrants
were like the North,
like the wind
or the waves …

When I get back to the wall
I'm tired.
Some come crying,
or they say nothing.
Everyone is tired.

I Dreamed

I fell asleep and I dreamed.
I dreamed I was flying,
I dreamed I was a song,
I dreamed I was a butterfly,
I dreamed I was a fish
and a wave.
I dreamed
the sweetest dream of all.
Instead of going to the North,
I went back to El Salvador.

Afterword

On October 30, 2018, I heard that a caravan of fellow citizens
from El Salvador was gathering at the Plaza Divino Salvador
del Mundo and planning to leave the following morning for the
United States. Over thirty-five years ago, I had done the same.
My heart, the heart of a refugee and immigrant, understood
what they were doing. That evening, I visited the public square
to share a cup of coffee with them, some pan dulce, a word of
encouragement … The hundreds of Salvadorans who had
arrived were willing to undertake the long and dangerous walk
of over 2,500 miles (4,000 km) to reach the Tijuana border to
the United States. They were willing to risk their lives and
those of their children.

"We prefer to die trying than to die of hunger here, or have
the gangs kill us," said one woman. Most of the people were
from the countryside. Those who brought luggage had a small
bag, a sweater or jacket, and the hope of making it to the United
States — to the North. They also hoped that, once there, the
reasons that had forced them to flee El Salvador would be heard
and judged sufficient to allow them to remain as refugees and
rebuild their lives. The immigrants carried with them the hope
of meeting generous people along the way. Fortunately, they
did. In Mexico and Guatemala, people offered them shelter
and humanitarian support to allow them to continue their long
walk north.

I ask myself what people like Misael Martínez, his family and
the thousands of Central American immigrants are doing in
Tijuana. Despite the great obstacles to enter the United States,
some of them must have kept going. Others must have found

work while they wait for their requests for refugee status to be resolved. Others must be tired of all the uncertainty and not know what to do: whether to continue waiting in Tijuana, and make it to the North one day, or to return to their countries. I wonder what Misael is planning to do …

I've written this text in my eagerness to share the voices of hope, of anguish, of the thousands of immigrants from Central America who abandon our countries because of all the violence and the lack of opportunities. In their midst, I saw people who were hard workers, humble, desperate and tired of suffering.

Jorge Argueta

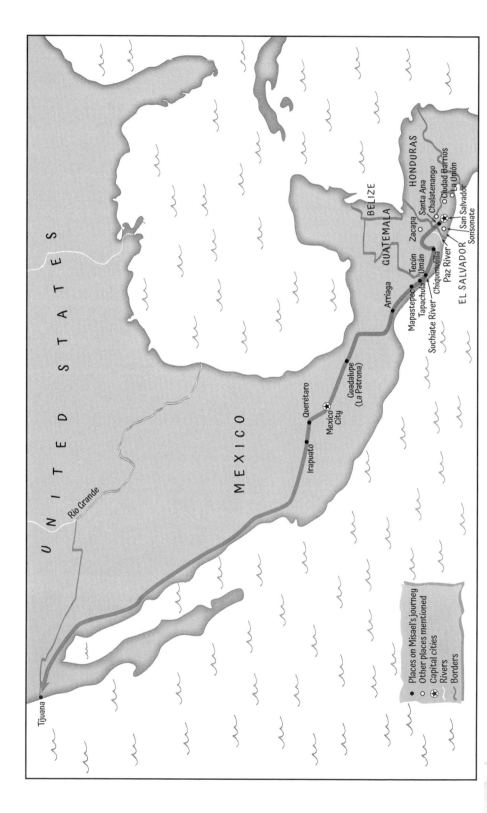